Una
the Concert Fairy

To Orren and Myah with love

Special thanks to
Rachel Elliot

ORCHARD BOOKS
338 Euston Road, London NW1 3BH
Orchard Books Australia
Level 17/207 Kent Street, Sydney, NSW 2000
A Paperback Original

First published in 2012 by Orchard Books

HiT entertainment

A CIP catalogue record for this book is available
from the British Library.

ISBN 978 1 40831 595 8

3 5 7 9 10 8 6 4

Printed in Great Britain

The paper and board used in this paperback are natural recyclable
products made from wood grown in sustainable forests. The
manufacturing processes conform to the environmental regulations
of the country of origin.

Orchard Books is a division of Hachette Children's Books,
an Hachette UK company

www.hachette.co.uk

Una
the Concert Fairy

by Daisy Meadows

ORCHARD

www.rainbowmagic.co.uk

Jack Frost's Ice Castle

Camping site

Girls' tent

Main Stage

Karaoke tent

Cafe

The Harbour

Rainspell Island

Jack Frost's Spell

It's high time for the world to see
The legend I was born to be.
The prince of pop, a dazzling star
My fans will flock from near and far.

But pop star fame is hard to get
Unless I help myself, I bet.
I need a plan, a cunning trick
To make my stage act super-slick.

Seven magic clefs I'll steal
They'll give me pop star powers, I feel.
I'll sing and dance, I'll dazzle and shine
And pop star glory will be mine!

Contents

Trouble on Rainspell Island

"My autograph book is almost full," said Kirsty Tate, turning the blue pages happily. "We've met so many famous pop stars at the festival!"

"Mine too," said Rachel Walker, who had her pink autograph book open on her lap. "I can't believe it's our last day already."

"The Rainspell Island Music Festival has been so much fun, I can hardly imagine going back to ordinary life," said Kirsty with a laugh. "I wish it didn't have to end."

Kirsty and Rachel were sitting on camping stools outside their tent. They had really enjoyed being special guests of their favourite pop group, The Angels. The afternoon sun seemed to light up the tents around them with a golden glow.

"It looks as if it's enchanted, doesn't it?" said Rachel.

"Almost as magical as the fairy campsite we visited with Jessie the Lyrics Fairy."

Kirsty and Rachel were good friends with many fairies, and they had often visited Fairyland and thwarted Jack Frost's schemes. On the first day of the festival, they had stumbled across one of his most mischievous plans yet. The Ice Lord had stolen seven magical clef necklaces from the Pop Star Fairies to try to become a pop star himself.

He had given most of the clefs to his goblins, who brought them to the Rainspell Island Festival, where Kirsty and Rachel had been able to track them down one by one. Jack Frost had disguised himself as rapper Jax Tempo to impress people at the festival, but he didn't fool the girls for long.

The Pop Star Fairies needed their clefs to look after all aspects of pop music, and Kirsty and Rachel were determined to help their friends. So far, they had helped six fairies get their magic clefs back, but Jack Frost still had one. It belonged to Una the Concert Fairy.

"I just hope that we can find the last clef before the end of the festival," said Kirsty. "Perhaps we should go and look for Una."

"But Queen Titania always says that we should wait for the magic to come to us," Rachel reminded her, turning another page of her autograph book.

"Just look at all the amazing people we've met this week, Kirsty. Dakota May, Jacob Bright, A-OK, Sasha Sharp, Groove Gang… and weren't all the concerts wonderful!"

"Yes, and tonight's concert will be the best yet," said Kirsty. "There's even going to be a surprise pop star. I hope that we can stop Jack Frost from spoiling it."

Just then, The Angels came strolling around the side of the tent. They were wearing long floral dresses, and had flowers twined in their hair.

"Hi, girls," said Lexy. "We're on our way to see the main stage being set up for tonight's concert. Would you like to come along?"

Rachel and Kirsty both smiled.

"Definitely!" they said together.

"Let's go!" said Emilia with a grin.

The girls and The Angels made their way out of the campsite area and through the festival site.

"The main stage is always super-busy," said Serena as they strolled past the exciting activity tents in Star Village. "I love the hustle and bustle of the roadies setting up the sound systems and the stars rehearsing."

It sounded wonderful! They passed the Food Fest picnic area and walked around a large tree.

"Here we are!" said Lexy.

But they were in for a big surprise. The stage was empty! No one was setting up for the concert and no one was rehearsing. Several roadies were standing around at the sides of the stage, looking very gloomy indeed. Melody Jones, the festival organiser, walked across the stage towards the girls, her face serious.

"Melody, what's wrong?" asked Emilia, leading the others up onto the stage.

"I'm afraid the electricity isn't working," Melody replied.

"That means no lights, no sound and *no concert!*"

At that moment there was a strange, cracking noise from backstage. Then they heard a loud bang, and a fountain of water sprayed onto the stage!

Rachel, Kirsty and The Angels darted backwards. Melody screamed as a wave of water rolled towards them.

"A pipe must have burst!" Serena exclaimed. "Let's get off this stage!"

They all hurried down to the front row of the stands.

"That was close!" said Emilia.

"What are we going to do?" poor Melody cried.

She was panicking, but The Angels stayed calm.

"We'll have to move the concert to another part of the festival," said Lexy. "Melody, is there somewhere else we can use?"

Before Melody could reply, her mobile phone rang. She answered it and her face fell.

"Looks as if it's bad news again," Rachel whispered.

"What's happened now?" asked Serena.

"Our special guest for tonight's finale has a sore throat and can't sing!" said Melody.

A Frosty Performance

Just then, Rachel noticed something at the side of the stage. One of the spotlights seemed to be giving out a tiny pool of light. She gently touched Kirsty's arm.

"Look over there," she whispered. "How can the spotlight be working if there's no electricity?"

"It must be magic," said Kirsty in excitement. "Come on, let's investigate."

Melody and The Angels were busy discussing how to save the festival finale, so they didn't notice the girls heading over to the spotlight. As Rachel and Kirsty drew closer, the little light darted away from them and into the stands at the side. The girls weaved in and out of the stands until they were out of sight of the others. Then the beam of light seemed to grow, before dissolving in a puff of rainbow-coloured fairy dust. A tiny fairy was fluttering in front of them. She was wearing a pretty orange dress with purple spangled tights.

"It's Una the Concert Fairy!" said Kirsty. "Hello!"

"Hi, girls!" said Una, flashing them a big smile.

She had a light sprinkling of freckles across her cheeks and nose, and her red-gold hair was thickly braided.

"We were hoping you'd find us," said Rachel. "It's the last day of the festival."

"I know," said Una. "I must get my magic clef back before tonight's concert. Without it, the finale of the Rainspell Island Music Festival will be ruined!"

"Things are already going wrong," said Rachel. "There's no electricity here, and a pipe has burst backstage."

"Oh my goodness," said Una, looking upset. "Girls, will you help me look for the clef?'

"Of course we will," Kirsty promised. "Let's go and find out what Melody is going to do."

Una flitted into the pocket of Rachel's denim jacket and the girls went back to the front row of the stands.

"I suppose you're right," Lexy was saying to Melody, looking very disappointed. "It's just such a pity for the festival to end like this, after such a happy week."

"What do you mean?" asked Rachel.

Melody and The Angels turned to look at the girls.

"We're going to have to cancel the final concert," Serena explained. "With no electricity and no special guest, everyone is just going to have to go home early."

Suddenly, they heard the squeal of an electric guitar. A haze of dry ice rose from the stage floor. Then the stage lights went on, and they saw a spiky-haired figure in a glittering ice-blue jacket striking a pose on top of a speaker.

"The electricity's back on!" cried Melody in relief.

"It's Jack Frost!" Kirsty whispered.

He was dressed in his Jax Tempo disguise. As the girls watched, he leapt off the speaker. Behind him, his band strutted onto the stage. They were wearing glittering green suits, and their enormous shiny green shoes were glistening under the spotlights.

"It's the goblins!" said Rachel. "What is Jack Frost up to now?"

Jax Tempo bounded across the stage, performing the rap that Kirsty and Rachel had heard before.

"I'm no fool
It's the number one rule,
I'm super-cool!"

His dancing
was wonderful,
and his sense
of rhythm
and timing
was perfect.
Behind him,
his goblin
band threw
themselves
into fast,
complicated
breakdancing moves.

"I know that he's up to no good,"
Kirsty whispered, "but he's putting on a
fabulous show."

Rachel nodded and glanced across at
The Angels. They were dancing along to
the music.

"He's great!" Lexy said.

Jack Frost jumped
back onto the
speaker and
thrashed out a
long final riff on
his guitar. He
ended his rap
on a spectacular
high, and as the
final note rang
out, everyone who
was watching burst into applause.

"Wonderful!" Melody exclaimed. "Jax, I want you to star in our festival finale – your performance was incredible!"

"I'll be there!" said Jack Frost with a wicked grin. He leapt up again and then slid along the floor on his knees, strumming his electric guitar in triumph.

Kirsty noticed a necklace bouncing over the guitar strap on Jack Frost's chest. It was a musical clef!

"Rachel, Jack Frost has the clef around his neck!" she whispered.

Pop Picnic

"Jack Frost might be a great performer, but it's only because he's stolen Una's magic clef," said Rachel. "It's not fair on the other bands!"

"We've got to get it back," said Kirsty in a determined voice.

"Girls, we're going to the festival office to finalise the concert arrangements," said Emilia. "We'll see you later, OK?"

"OK," called the girls.

They waited until Melody and The Angels had gone, and then they walked up onto the stage. Jack Frost had his back to them. Kirsty folded her arms across her chest and Rachel put her hands on her hips.

"Jax!" said Rachel. Jack Frost whirled around. When he saw the girls, he scowled horribly.

"Not you two again!" he said. "Clear off, now!"

"Don't forget, we know who you really are," said Kirsty.

"*And* we know how you are putting on such a great performance," Rachel added. "That clef doesn't belong to you, so give it back to Una."

"No chance!" snarled Jack Frost. "This is my big break, and you can't stop me. The world deserves to know about Jax Tempo!"

Before the girls could reply, he sent bolt after bolt of icy magic flying towards them. Kirsty and Rachel dived aside as Jack Frost jumped off the stage and sprinted away.

The goblins followed
him as fast as they
could, pushing
and shoving
each other, and
squawking with
laughter.

"He told you!"
giggled a spotty
goblin as he
barged past Rachel.

"Go away, pesky humans!" yelled
another.

"Let's follow them!" Rachel cried,
running down the stage steps. "Come
on, Kirsty, we can't let them get
away now!"

The girls chased after the disappearing
goblins and their bad-tempered boss.

"They're heading into the festival area!" panted Kirsty. "Faster, Rachel, we're going to lose them!"

They saw a glittery green leg disappearing around the corner of a hot-dog stand. But when they raced around the stand, both Jack Frost and the goblins had

vanished. Una popped her head out of Rachel's jacket pocket.

"Find somewhere to hide out of sight," she said. "We'll find them much more quickly if you two are fairies as well."

They ducked behind a souvenir kiosk
and Una fluttered out of Rachel's
pocket. She raised her wand and flew
around Rachel and Kirsty, scattering
rainbow-coloured fairy dust. It tickled as
it landed lightly on them, and lifted them
into the air, surrounding them in a whirl
of colour. They shrank to fairy size, and
beautiful gossamer wings
appeared on their
shoulders.

"Oh I love
being a fairy!"
said Rachel,
delightedly
looping the loop.

"Me too," Kirsty
replied, twirling
into the air.

"I'm glad," said Una with a laugh.
"Come on, let's find Jack Frost and stop
him from causing any more trouble!"

The three friends swooped high into
the sky and looked down at the bustling
crowds of the festival. It was a
wonderful sight.

"There's so much going on down
there," said Rachel. "Look at all
the colours!"

"Yes," said Kirsty. "Lots of reds and
yellows and *greens*. How are we going
to spot the goblins among all those
people?"

"Look over there," said Una, pointing
to the Food Fest area. "Why is that
crowd gathering? Perhaps the goblins are
putting on another performance!"

"Let's find out," said Rachel.

They zoomed
down and hid
among the
leaves of a tree
close to the
crowd. The
people were
standing around
a large picnic blanket,
where A-OK, Sasha Sharp, Groove
Gang, Dakota May and Jacob Bright
were all having a picnic together.

"Some of the best pop stars from the
festival are here," said Kirsty. "No
wonder they've attracted such a crowd.
Ooh, this gives me a great idea for the
finale concert!"

"But first we have to find Una's clef,"
said Rachel.

The picnic looked like great fun. The pop stars were singing and jamming together, and it was almost like a mini concert! The girls were enjoying listening to the music, but then Rachel gave an exclamation.

"Look – at the edge of the crowd!"

She pointed at a flash of ice blue darting through the crowd, followed by several flashes of green.

"It's Jack Frost and the goblins!" cried Una.

"I've got an idea," Rachel said. "Una, can you use your magic to make your voice sound as if it's in the crowd? Jack Frost will stop if he thinks there are fans around him!"

"Let's try it!" said Kirsty.

Disguise for Danger

Una tapped her wand against her throat and chanted a spell.

"To stop the mischief Jack began,
Make me sound just like a fan!"

A ribbon of fairy dust wound from the tip of her wand and circled her neck. When she spoke again, her voice sounded as if it came from somewhere in the crowd.

"Look, there's Jax Tempo!" she shouted. "He's in the ice-blue jacket! I heard that he's the surprise star at tonight's finale! Let's get his autograph!"

The people who were standing around the pop stars' picnic turned to Jack Frost, who stopped in his tracks. He grinned and waved at them all.

"Hello, fans!" he said with a simpering giggle. "I know I'm brilliant. Try not to faint with excitement, now!"

The goblins elbowed people out of the way, clearing a path for Jack Frost like bodyguards.

"Stand clear, out of the star's personal space!" they shouted. "Make way! Make way! The famous Jax Tempo is coming through!"

"Let's follow them!" said Kirsty.

The three fairies flew out from the leaves and hid behind a fluttering flag, close to where Jack Frost and his goblins were showing off.

"We just have to swoop down and get the clef while he's distracted," said Rachel.

"That's easier said than done," said Una in a worried voice. "There are hundreds of people milling about – we'd be spotted if we flew down there now."

"We'll just have to wait until he's alone," said Kirsty.

Jack Frost was making his way towards his trailer. He gave a final smile and a wave, and then disappeared into the trailer with his goblins. As the door slammed, the three fairies exchanged looks of despair.

"How are we going to get the magic clef now?" groaned Una. "Even if we could get into the trailer without being seen, it's absolutely *full* of goblins!"

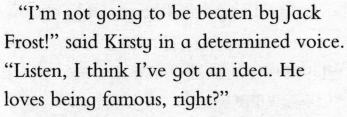

"I'm not going to be beaten by Jack Frost!" said Kirsty in a determined voice. "Listen, I think I've got an idea. He loves being famous, right?"

"Right," agreed Una and Rachel.

"I bet that he'd love to be on TV," Kirsty continued. "How about we disguise ourselves as goblins and pretend that we want to film him for a goblin TV show? He might let us into the trailer, and then at least we'll have a chance to get the clef back."

Una looked doubtful.

"That could be really dangerous," she said. "What if he sees through the disguise? We could be trapped in the trailer with him."

"I think it's worth the risk," said Rachel bravely. "If we don't get that clef back, Jax Tempo will be the only act on the stage tonight. We're not going to let that happen!"

"Thank you!" said Una. "I'm so grateful to you both."

The three friends flew down to the trailer and hid in the long grass behind it.

They checked that no one was
looking, and then Una waved her wand.
Instantly, Kirsty and Rachel grew to
goblin size. They looked
at each other and
giggled. Their
skin was turning
green, and
their ears were
growing long
and pointy.

Kirsty had a
microphone in
her hand and was
disguised as a goblin
TV reporter. Rachel was carrying a
goblin-sized camera on her right
shoulder. Each of them was wearing a
peaked cap with 'GOBLIN TV' on it.

"You look terrible!" said Rachel with a squawky goblin laugh.

"You too!" Kirsty chuckled.

Una tucked herself under Kirsty's cap, and then the girls walked around to the front of the trailer and knocked on the door. It was opened by one of Jack Frost's backing dancers.

"What do you want?" he snapped at them.

"Hi, we're here from Goblin TV," said Rachel. "We want an exclusive interview with Jack Frost.

It'll be beamed to every single goblin, and everyone will know about the famous Jax Tempo!"

The goblin's mouth fell open, and there was a sudden excited chatter from the goblins inside the trailer.

"You let them in – right now!" roared Jack Frost's voice.

The goblin on the door stepped aside, and Kirsty and Rachel walked into the trailer. It was dark inside, and it smelled of bad breath and old socks. When their eyes adjusted to the light, they saw Jack Frost lying back on a blue chaise longue. The goblins were squatting around him and popping grapes into his mouth.

"Camera rolling," said Rachel, zooming in on Jack Frost's face.

"So what's it like living the life of a famous pop star?" asked Kirsty, sticking her microphone under Jack Frost's nose.

"Fantastic – the silly humans adore me!" said Jack with a sneer. "I've got what it takes to make it all the way to the top, and no one's going to stop me!"

"And could you explain for the viewers how you cleverly stole the magical clefs from the Pop Star Fairies?" asked Kirsty.

"It was a work of genius!" Jack Frost boasted. "I sneaked into their dressing room while the fairies were trying on their silly outfits. Ha ha!"

Rachel and Kirsty could only manage weak giggles at this.

"Er, could I get a close-up of the clef you're wearing, for the viewers?" asked Rachel, hoping that he would take the necklace off for her.

"No problem," said Jack Frost.

He held out the clef on its chain, without taking it off. Rachel glanced at Kirsty as she filmed the clef. What were they going to do now?

Goblin Traitors!

"So, Jack, what would you say to your critics?" asked Kirsty, thinking fast.

"Critics?" he snarled, sitting up very straight. "What critics?"

The other goblins backed away and huddled in a corner of the trailer.

"Well, some goblins are saying that you're only a pop star because of the magic clef," Kirsty explained, shrugging her shoulders. "They say that without it you'd be a dreadful singer."

The goblins in the corner gave scared gasps, and Kirsty held her breath. It was very dangerous to make Jack Frost angry. "That's not true!" he bellowed, pulling the necklace off and scowling at Kirsty. "I don't need magic to be brilliant – I've got the Frost Factor and I'm going to prove it!"

"What do you mean?" Rachel asked.

"Hold this," said Jack Frost, thrusting the necklace into Kirsty's hand. "I'll sing my song without the clef, and you'll see that I don't need those pesky fairies to be a star!"

He jumped up and started to sing:

"I'm no fool
It's the number one rule,
I'm super-cool!"

Rachel clapped her hands over her ears. His rapping sounded like nails being dragged down a blackboard. Kirsty saw his eyes widen – he knew how bad he sounded.

"Now, Una!" she cried.

Una fluttered out from under her cap and put her hands on the magical clef. As soon as she touched it, it shrank to fairy size. Jack Frost stopped singing and gave a howl of rage.

"What are you doing?" he yelled. "Traitors! Since when have goblins helped fairies? Have you gone mad? I'll turn you into toadstools for this!"

"They're not goblins,"
said Una, glaring at
him. "They're
two very brave
human beings!"

With a wave
of her wand, the
goblin disguises
melted away. Jack
Frost jumped up and hopped around the
trailer in a towering temper.

"You interfering humans!" he
screeched. "You nosy little fairy! I never
wanted to perform in your stupid concert
finale anyway. I'll have my revenge on
you all for this!"

"It's your own fault," said Rachel.
"You stole the Pop Star Fairies' clefs, and
that was wrong."

"You can't tell me what to do!" Jack Frost shouted. "I've had enough of the Rainspell Island Festival. We're going back to the Ice Castle – *right now*! Goblins, you're coming with me!"

Jack Frost stood in the centre of the trailer and clicked his fingers, expecting the goblins to scurry to his side. But none of them moved.

"Now!" he bellowed. "We don't need stupid music festivals and stupid pop songs."

"But I've been having fun," whined one of the goblins. "I don't want to leave!"

"I like it here," complained another goblin. "Why do we have to go?"

"WHAT?" hollered Jack Frost. "I'll make you sorry for disobeying me! I'll make you wish you'd never heard of pop music!"

"Let's get out of here!" said Una, fluttering towards the door.

While Jack Frost was shouting, Kirsty, Rachel and Una slipped away. They could still hear his bellows when they reached the main concert stage.

"We have to tell The Angels that they've lost their star performer," said Rachel. "Jax Tempo has disappeared – hopefully forever! I feel sorry for The Angels though. They've been working so hard to make this concert a success."

"I've had an idea about that," said Kirsty with a grin. Melody and The Angels were on the stage, managing the roadies who were testing the sound system.

"Hi, girls!" said Serena, smiling at them.

"Hi, Serena," said Kirsty. "We've got good news and bad news…"

At first Melody and The Angels were worried when they heard that Jax Tempo had gone home. But when Kirsty explained her idea, their faces brightened.

"I thought of it when I saw all the pop stars having a picnic together," she said. "How about putting all the acts on stage together?"

"That could work!" said Melody.

"I think it's a great idea," said Emilia. "There's been nothing like that at the festival before – it'll be amazing!"

"I'd better start organising it then," said Melody with a smile. "Thanks, Kirsty!"

The girls went back to Una, who was waiting for them in the empty stands. Her eyes were sparkling with excitement.

"Girls, you've done so much to help me and the other Pop Star Fairies," she said. "Now that I have my clef back, the Fairyland Music Festival can go ahead. Would you like to come as our guests of honour?"

"Yes, please!" said Rachel and Kirsty.

They both loved going to Fairyland, and it was even more exciting now that they knew all seven clefs were safe. They knew that time would stand still in the human world while they were visiting the fairies, so no one would miss them while they were away.

Una waved her wand and a glittering bubble surrounded the girls. It lifted them into the air, gently spinning. Then it popped in a puff of fairy dust, and Rachel and Kirsty found themselves in the royal box at the Fairyland Music Festival!

Festival Fun!

"Welcome, Rachel!" said a musical voice beside the girls. "Welcome, Kirsty!"

The girls turned and saw that they were sitting next to Queen Titania and King Oberon.

"Once again, you have proved yourselves loyal friends of Fairyland," said King Oberon. "This is going to be a wonderful festival – thanks to you."

"It's starting!" said the queen.

The stage looked magnificent, with lights of every colour and garlands of flowers looped around the equipment. The stands were filled with excited fairies, whose gauzy wings glimmered in the sunlight. Spotlights swept across the crowd, and cheers went up as a very stylish-looking fairy appeared on the stage.

"It's Destiny the Pop Star Fairy!" said Rachel.

"Welcome to the Fairyland Music Festival!" Destiny announced. "It's great to see you all here – especially our guests of honour, Rachel and Kirsty.

Without them, there wouldn't even be a festival!"

The crowd cheered again, and Rachel and Kirsty smiled and waved. They could see lots of their friends watching from the stands.

"So," Destiny went on, "without any further ado, put your hands together for... the Showtime Fairies!"

It was a wonderful concert. The Showtime Fairies, the Music Fairies and the Dance Fairies all performed, as well as a host of other unforgettable acts. Kirsty and Rachel clapped until their hands were sore!

Halfway through the concert, Rachel nudged Kirsty.

"Look over there," she said with a surprised smile.

At the back of the audience, they could see Jack Frost and his goblins. They were still wearing their festival outfits. Jack Frost was scowling and his arms were folded across his chest, but one of his big feet was tapping in time to the music.

The concert was a huge success. Best of all was the grand finale, when all the Pop Star Fairies performed together with Destiny.

The show ended with fireworks exploding from the front of the stage, and then the Pop Star Fairies fluttered up to the royal box and hovered in front of the girls.

"Thank you all so much," said Una. "We couldn't have done any of this without you."

"It was our pleasure!" said Rachel.

They hugged each of the Pop Star Fairies, and then Queen Titania stood up to speak.

"It has been wonderful to have you here as our guests," she said. "But now it is time to send you back to Rainspell Island. You have another festival finale to enjoy."

She waved her wand, and the stands and fairies around them seemed to melt away. Rachel and Kirsty were caught up in a golden whirlpool, and when it finally disappeared they were back on Rainspell Island.

That evening at the final concert of the Rainspell Island Music Festival, Rachel and Kirsty were standing in the front row with Rachel's parents, cheering and dancing along to the music. The stage was full of famous pop stars for the last performance of the concert.

"Rachel! Kirsty!" called Melody, dashing towards them from the side of the stage. "How would you like to go up on stage with all of the pop stars for the finale?"

The girls nodded eagerly, and a few seconds later they were standing in a line between Dakota May and Jacob Bright. Everyone had their arms around each other's shoulders, and the atmosphere was electric. The moon shone down on them as they sang a final song.

"It's like magic!
Let's work together to get the job done.
It's like magic!
If we help one another, we'll have lots
of fun."

As the last notes of the song rang out
and the audience burst into deafening
applause, Rachel looked across the sea
of faces. She saw her parents beaming
with pride in the front row, and waved
at them.

As the applause died away, The Angels stepped forwards.

"We would like to offer a very special thank-you to two important people," said Lexy.

"Just a few hours ago, it was looking as if the final concert would have to be cancelled," Emilia added.

"But thanks to Rachel and Kirsty, this finale has been the best I've ever seen!" finished Serena. "Take a bow, Rachel Walker and Kirsty Tate!"

Feeling shy but very proud, the girls

stepped forward and bowed to the audience. The pop stars gathered around them and burst into a final encore, and Rachel and Kirsty exchanged happy smiles as the audience cheered.

"A fairy festival and a pop concert all in one night," said Kirsty, squeezing her best friend's hand. "Isn't this amazing!"

"We are so lucky," Rachel agreed. "Oh Kirsty, I don't think summer holidays get any better than this!"

**Now Kirsty and Rachel
must help…**

Miranda the Beauty Fairy

Read on for a sneak peek…

"This is amazing, Rachel!" Kirsty exclaimed. Her eyes wide, she stared up at the enormous glittering steel and glass building in front of them. Across the entrance was *Tippington Fountains Shopping Centre* in blue lights.

"Yes, isn't it?" Rachel agreed. "I'm so glad you're staying with me for half-term so that you could be here for the grand opening, Kirsty."

"Me, too," Kirsty said eagerly. "And I'm really looking forward to seeing Jessica Jarvis!" The famous supermodel

Jessica Jarvis was the star guest at the new shopping centre's opening ceremony. Crowds of people had already gathered, waiting for the ceremony to begin.

"I think we're just in time for the parade," Mrs Walker said, locking her car. "Come along, girls."

Rachel, Kirsty and Mrs Walker hurried to join the crowd. Moments later the first float appeared around the side of the building.

"Every shop in the mall has its own float, Kirsty," Rachel explained. "Look, the first one is *Tippington Toys*."

The float rumbled slowly towards them. A huge inflatable teddy bear sat on the back of the truck, and also on the float were girls dressed as rag dolls with yellow wool pigtails and flouncy dresses, and boys wearing red soldier uniforms.

They waved to the crowds as they passed by.

"The next one is *The Book Nook*," Kirsty said, reading the painted banner strung across the float.

The *Book Nook* float carried people dressed as characters from storybooks. The girls spotted Snow White, Cinderella, Pinocchio and several others. This was followed by the *Sweet Scoop Ice Cream Parlour* float with its giant foam ice-cream cones.

"Those ice creams look lovely!" Kirsty laughed.

Rachel sniffed the air. "I can smell something lovely, too," she said...

Read Miranda the Beauty Fairy to find out what adventures are in store for Kirsty and Rachel!

Meet the fairies, play games
and get sneak peeks at
the latest books!

www.rainbowmagicbooks.co.uk

There's fairy fun for everyone on
our wonderful website.
You'll find great activities, competitions, stories and
fairy profiles, and also a special newsletter.

Get 30% off all Rainbow Magic books at
www.rainbowmagicbooks.co.uk

Enter the code RAINBOW at the checkout.
Offer ends 31 December 2013.

Offer valid in United Kingdom and Republic of Ireland only.

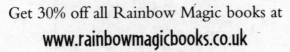

Look out for the next sparkly
Rainbow Magic Special!

Robyn the Christmas Party Fairy

Rachel and Kirsty are helping to organise a big Christmas party.
But Jack Frost has stolen Robyn the Christmas Party Fairy's
magical objects! The girls must help Robyn,
before the spirit of Christmas is lost forever...

Out now!

Alexandra
the Royal Baby
Fairy

Out in May 2013

 Also available as an ebook

The whole of Fairyland is very excited - there's going to be a new royal baby! But when the special baby goes missing, Rachel and Kirsty are there to help their friend, Alexandra the Royal Baby Fairy.

www.rainbowmagicbooks.co.uk

Meet the
Princess Fairies

Honor
the Happy Days
Fairy

Demi
the Dressing-Up
Fairy

Anya
the Cuddly Creatures
Fairy

Elisa
the Adventure
Fairy

Lizzie
the Sweet Treats
Fairy

Maddie
the Fun and Games
Fairy

Eva
the Enchanted Ball
Fairy

**Jack Frost has stolen the Princess Fairies'
tiaras. Kirsty and Rachel must get them back
before all the magic in the world fades away!**

www.rainbowmagicbooks.co.uk